THE RED SEA SHARKS

It's extraordinary! Imagine! The Captain and I were just this moment talking about you!

Qué? . . . Of me?

Yes, of you . . . weren't we, Captain? Then up you pop like a jack-in-a-box. It's incredible . . . But tell me, General, what are you doing nowadays?

Me? . . . Er . . . Well . . . Si . . . I . . . travel . . . But . . .

Por favor . . . excuse please . . . In mucho hurry . . . Already late for appointment . . . I go now.

Oh, what a pity . . . At all events, here's my address. And where can we find you, General?

Er . . . Um . . . At thees hotel . . . er . . . thees Hotel Bristol.

Good! The Bristol . . . And when do you . . .

Just so . . . Now I go . . . Adios, amigos!

Goodbye, General.

Well, well! Frankly, I don't think your friend Alcazar was in a very chatty mood!

Yes, an odd fellow. Oh well, come on.

? OH!

Crumbs! It's the general's wallet. He didn't put it right inside his pocket.

Quick! He can't have got far.

Hello, where's he gone to? . . .

Perhaps he got into a car . . . Never mind. The Hotel Bristol is quite near; we'll leave his wallet there.

A few minutes later, at the Bristol . . .

General Alcazar? . . . No, Sir, we have no one of that name here.

I wonder: perhaps he's registered under another name . . . Ramon Zarate? . . .

Ramon Zarate? . . . No, sir. A Spanish gentleman?

South American. Quite well-built. A long chin . . . small moustache . . . Wait, I'll try to draw him for you.

There . . . That's about it . . .

No, sir. I'm terribly sorry, but I don't know the gentleman.

Oh? That's odd. Well, thank you.

BRIST

Now what can we do to return that idiot's wallet to him?

That's what I'm wondering.

I say, why shouldn't the wallet itself give us a clue towards finding the general. Come on; we'll go in here.

Bring us . . . er . . . let's see . . . let's see . . .

Two glasses of ginger beer.

Now then, let's see what's inside here.

ROSSINI

Pound notes, French and Belgian money, a hotel bill, a four-leaf clover, a lottery ticket from San Theodoros . . . in fact, nothing to give us a lead.

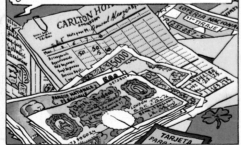

. . . And in this envelope, photos of aircraft . . . Odd, isn't it, Captain?

Ah, a letter! . . . This time I think we're on to something. Look, Captain.

Friday

bear Sir,

Please telephone PIC 8524 between 10. and 12.0 p.m. Ask for Mr. Debrett

Regards,
J.D.M.C.

But the general's address isn't here.

I know, but I'll ring up the number given in the letter.

ROSSINI

Hello, is that PIC 8524? May I speak to Mr Debrett? . . . Who am I? . . . A friend of General Alcazar, and I . . . Hello? . . . HELLO?? . . .

Can you hear me? . . . What? . . . You don't know the name Alcazar? . . . What about Ramon Zarate? . . . Nor that? . . . You see, sir, I found his wallet and . . . I beg your pardon?

I tell you, sir, I am not Mr Debrett! I don't know your General Alhambra, and I am not interested in your story . . . Goodbye!

There's politeness for you! . . .

Very odd . . . They don't know of him at that number. Too bad . . . We'd better be getting home to Marlinspike.

A little later . . .

How strange. The front door's open . . .

WOOAAAH! . . . WOOAAAH! . . .

?   ?

Good heavens! My poor Snowy! Who's done this to you?!

I'll get to the bottom of it!

Hey, Captain, what's happened to you?

Billions of blue blistering barnacles! Who's the thundering son of a sea-gherkin who did that? . . . Nestor! . . . Nestor!

HAAAAH! . . .

Th . . . th . . . th . . . there behind you!

!? RRHOAH! . . .

ABDULLAH! . . . WRAOUH!

ABDULLAH? . . .

ABDULLAH! . . .

Abdullah! Blistering . . .

Again, Blistering Barnacles! Fall downstairs again!

You young ruffian! Just you tell me what you're doing here!

Wait! . . . Wait, Blistering Barnacles! I've got something for you.

Something for me?

Yes, a present.

A present! . . . Something specially for me, brought from his country, I expect. Dear little fellow!

It's for you, Blistering Barnacles, from me.

Thank you, Abdullah.

A cuckoo-clock! Why, it's magnificent, Abdullah!

You see . . . to wind it up . . .

. . . you do that!

Ten thousand thundering typhoons! . . . Don't think you'll get away with that!

WAAAH! WAAAH!

Halt thou! . . . Touch not the son of my Master!

? ?

Me Hassim, servant to His Highness Prince Abdullah . . .

And I bring you message from my Master.

Most esteemed and well-beloved friend,

I entrust to you my son Abdullah, to improve his English. Here the situation is serious. Should any misfortune befall me I count on you, my friend, to care for Abdullah.

Emir Ben-Kalish Ezab

Read that, Tintin, it's for you . . . Tell me Hassim, what does the Emir mean . . . "the situation is serious"?

I know not, Effendi.

What d'you make of it? One thing's clear: we've got Abdullah on our hands. We'll have to bring the young scamp to heel.

Abdullah! . . . You little brat! I'm going to teach you a lesson . . .

WAAH!

Halt thou! . . . Touch not the son of my Master!

Touch not! Touch not! You arabesque, you! D'you imagine I'm going to let that little pest raise Cain in my house?

Just wait till I find you, you young rapscallion!

Oh sir! . . . Sir! . . . It's terrible, sir . . . All those foreign persons have settled themselves . . .

Later, Nestor . . . tell me later.

. . . in the state-rooms!

The next morning . . .

RRRRING
RRRRING
?

HELLO?

Blue blistering barnacles in a thundering typhoon!

All right . . . All right! . . . I'm coming!

RRRING
RRRING

RRRING

Hello? . . . Hello? . . . Who? . . . What? . . . Who d'you want?! No, Madam. I am not Mr Cutts the butcher!

☆!!!+ ☺ ♂ ☆ ✹ ≸ ✹ ! ≫<☆ ᴍᴍ !

BLUB   BLUB
BLUB
BLUB
SPLOSH

RRRING

No answer? . . . I suppose they're all asleep still . . .

To be precise, I'd say . . .

HELLO!

Hello? . . . Who's that? Thompson? . . . What? . . . Oh yes, with a "p". Well?

I . . . I . . . I'm not disturbing you, am I?

Er . . . not in the least. Go on . . .

Is Tintin here this morning? . . . Yes. You'd like to speak to him? . . . Right . . . What? . . . Do we know General Alcazar? . . . Yes, why?

You'll explain that to Tintin later? Good . . . What? . . . No, no trouble at all . . .

Ringing up when I'm in the bath! I ask you!

Half an hour later . . .

Well, well! Thompson and Thomson? . . . And they want to talk to me about General Alcazar. Odd, isn't it?

Yes . . . Talking of odd things . . . where's Abdullah this morning?

KHRRR KHRRR

Blistering barnacles, here he comes!

No, it's Calculus!

Good gracious!

You goat, you! D'you often feel impelled to come to breakfast on roller-skates?

Very well, thanks. And you?

Now admit it. You're puzzled to see me come in like that . . . Yes, yes, you find it odd, don't deny it! . . . Well, I can't tell you anything more at present . . .

RRRRING

. . . but quite soon you'll see my reason for it.

The Thompsons? Already! . . .

Ah! . . . Now for some breakfast.

D'you think so?

You thundering nitwitted numbskull you! Haven't you finished acting the goat yet?

Who rang, Nestor?

I found no one the first time, sir. But the second time, I saw Abdullah running away.

I bet that's him! But he won't get away with it this time. Nestor, go and bring the hose-pipe!

Now . . . as soon as he rings, you open the door, and then: psshhtt! . . . We'll get a good laugh!

That's it! . . . Quick, open up, Nestor!

I . . . I'm dreadfully sorry! . . . Please forgive me! You see, it's Abdullah's fault. The young rapscallion kept ringing the bell . . .

Ha! ha! ha! ha!

A few minutes later . . .

Well, here's the position. Interpol have asked us to keep an eye on a man called Dawson, and to collect all the information we can about his activities . . .

. . . and also about the people he meets. It so happens that you know one of them: General Alcazar. What can you tell us about him?

Very little, as a matter of fact.

I knew him when he was President of the Republic of San Theodoros. I met him later, in Europe. He'd been deposed by his rival, General Tapioca, and had fled from his country. He'd become a knife-thrower on the music-halls . . .
That's all.

All? Really? And what did he say to you, when you met him last night?

9

Aha! That surprised you, eh? You forget, my friend, in our job there's nothing we don't know.

To be precise: we know nothing in our job!

It's true that we met him last night. I was going to tell you . . . He said he was travelling, he was in a hurry, and he was staying at the Hotel . . . er . . . the Hotel . . .

Excelsior; yes, we know.

Oh? Well, that's the lot . . . He didn't say anything else . . . But what have you against him? What do you suspect?

Why are we suspect? I mean, what do we suspect? My dear fellow, if you imagine we'll tell you he's smuggling aircraft, you're much mistaken. "Mum's the word", that's our motto.

Well said! . . . To be precise: "Dumb's the word", that's our motto. The general may have come to Europe to buy up old aircraft, but you won't learn that from us! Now we must be going. Goodbye, Tintin.

Goodbye.

Ah! Here comes Nestor with our hats and sticks.

What a very peculiar thing: my hat has shrunk.

How strange. With me it's the opposite; I've got a swollen head . . .

Oh, I see. We've got muddled up. You have my hat and I have yours.

That's it: our mats are in a huddle. In short, we're contrarywise . . .

But it still isn't right!

Nor is mine!

May I see? . . . You can bet Abdullah's behind this . . .

Abdullalah?

There! . . . I thought as much. It's an old joke: newspapers folded up and slipped into the band.

A little later on . . .

Abdullah and his tricks!

Well, what did our Siamese twins want?

?

Just read this advertisement I've found in an old newspaper!

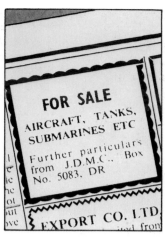

FOR SALE
AIRCRAFT, TANKS, SUBMARINES ETC
Further particulars from J.D.M.C., Box No. 5083, DR
EXPORT CO. LTD.

Extraordinary! . . . Why don't they add: "on easy terms". You'll see, we'll end up buying a battleship or the 'Queen Mary' on the never-never!

Maybe. But did you notice the initials?

J.D.M.C. . . . J.D.M.C. . . . Thundering typhoons! Alcazar's wallet! The signature on that letter!

Precisely!

No doubt about it: the general's here to buy armaments. But that's no reason for failing to return his wallet. And since Thompson and Thomson have kindly told us the right address . . .

I'll come with you.

Later, at the Hotel Excelsior . . .

General Alcazar? Yes, he's here, sir. I just saw him go past. You'll find him in the lounge.

Thank you.

There . . .

Look . . . he's talking to someone. But . . . good heavens! It's Dawson. I've met him before. He was police chief in the International Settlement in Shanghai.

And there in the background, lurking behind their newspapers . . .

The Thompsons!

This all looks pretty fishy; I'd like to know a bit more about it. Listen, Captain; you stay here, and as soon as Dawson goes, you return General Alcazar's wallet. I'll follow Dawson. We'll meet at Marlinspike.

OK

An hour later . . .

There he is . . . getting into that black Jaguar.

Quick, taxi! . . . Follow that black Jaguar, there, ahead of us.

Where are we off to now?

Fifteen minutes later . . .

We're on the outskirts of town already . . . Ah, he's slowing down. He's going to turn off.

This is it, driver. Stop!

Oh! A watchman!

How can I get in without being seen? . . . Perhaps . . . Yes, I know . . .

We're over the first hurdle. Now let's see . . .

Aircraft! So we were right!

Careful! Footsteps!

'Morning guv'. Seen the "Reporter" today? . . . No? Well, read that . . .

Aha! Bravo! . . . The Mosquitoes we sold them did a grand job. Those boys know how to make use of them!

How right you are! Any news from Alcazar?

It's in the bag! Twelve Mosquitoes there, too. To help him chuck out his rival, General Tapioca . . . Suits us. Let them fight. So long as we can unload our junk on them, why worry?

You've said it! . . . Well, I'll see to the packing of those DC3 spares for Arabair. Now that they've got the green light over there, they're going to need them. It looks to me . . .

RRRR RRRR

What's that? . . . What on earth's going on? . . . What's this confounded thing?

Where the devil's that row coming from?!

An alarm-clock!

Abdullah, the little pest! I'll bet he put that alarm-clock in my pocket!

A young lad with a white dog, you say? . . . How did they manage to get in without your seeing?

"Daily Reporter" sir . . .

Thanks.

CRUMBS!

Great Scot! What will the Captain think of this?

A little later . . .

A youngster with a white dog? That reminds me of something . . . but what?

RRRING RRRING

Hello? . . . Who's that? . . . Oh, it's you, General . . . What? . . . Oh, your wallet . . . You've got it back?

Yes, they bring him back. This Captain Haddock, who I meet yesterday with one of my friends . . . Tintin . . . Qué? . . . Si, Tintin. You know him? . . . Qué? The telephone call you receive last night? . . . Yes, it was him. He find your number in my wallet.

Tintin! . . . So he's the one sticking his nose into my business! . . . I'll soon take care of him . . .

The airport at Wadesdah, capital of Khemed, three days later . . .

Here comes the plane from Beirut.

You understand? If he's aboard, you put this briefcase in the baggage compartment.

WADESDAH AIRPORT

I'm not sorry to get here . . . With these old crates you can never be sure . . .

I say, have you noticed? . . . Armed men all over the place.

Passports, please gentlemen.

I am sorry, gentlemen: you have no permit to stay in Khemed. You must reboard the plane, and return to Beirut.

⑮

Golly! I can smell trouble. There's something sinister going on here. I must warn Tintin at once.

I'm wondering WHO warned the authorities at Wadesdah of our arrival, and WHO persuaded them to deport us?

Hello, Snowy, what's the matter?

WOOAH! WOOAH!

Here, will you stop that! You know, he . . . yes, he wants to show me something. All right, I'll follow you . . .

WOOAH! WOOAH!

In there? It's the luggage. You want me to go in? All right, I'm coming.

WOOAH! WOOAH!

PH-E-E-E-T

?

PH-E-E-E-T

What's that siren for?

الخريبقة

An engine on fire! That's the alarm for the extinguishers!

Thundering typhoons! The extinguishers haven't worked; it's burning more fiercely than ever!

Wadesdah Tower . . . Wadesdah Tower . . . This is KH-OZD . . . Starboard motor on fire . . . Extinguishers unserviceable. We're turning back . . . We'll try to reach Wadesdah.

It's no good! It's too heavy. I shall just have to . . .

TOCK TICK TICK TOCK TICK TOCK

17

My bottle! . . . I must save my bottle!

Thundering typhoons! The plane's blown up!

But my bottle's safe!

Columbus! . . . Tintin?

He went towards the plane . . . Let's hope . . . Careful: mustn't break my bottle . . .

TINTIN! . . . TINTIN! . . .

SMASH

Billions of blistering barnacles!

Tintin, old man! . . . You aren't broken? . . . I mean . . . you aren't hurt?

N . . . no. I was just knocked flat by the blast. But Snowy? Where's Snowy?

Safe and sound. He's fetching your hat.

Snowy, good old Snowy. You scented danger, eh? . . . And I just thought you wanted to play.

You know, Tintin, you ought to take me more seriously.

A time-bomb in the baggage compartment . . . So it's thanks to the fire in the starboard motor that we're still alive! . . . Normally, at this time, we'd be flying over the mountains, over the Jebel . . . You can imagine, if we'd blown up in the air . . .

Yes, we've had a lucky escape. I wonder . . .

What?

Nothing . . . but I think we won't hang around here. Let's go.

All right. I agree.

I always keep a small flask of rum for emergencies. Now's the time to use it . . .

This confounded cork won't come out . . .

Ah! . . . That's it!

POP

POP = 🍾 = 🍾 =WHISKY

Stop! That's enough!

Aaah! Now then, where are those sprouts? . . . I mean scouts . . . ? I'd l-l-like a word or two w-w-with them!

Sh! Be quiet! We must get on.

Early next day . . .

Wadesdah at last! Now we must be careful . . . The main gates will be watched; but I know a small gateway, and that'll be unguarded.

There, you see. We got in unmolested. Now we must find Senhor Oliveira de Figueira. I'm sure his house is near here.

Yes, that's it. I remember.

You did say he always has a bottle of wine handy?

Senhor Oliveira! . . . Senhor Oliveira! . . .

The joke's on us if he's moved!

Senhor Oliveira! . . . Senhor Oliveira! . . . Open the door! It's Tintin!

?

Blistering barnacles! . . . A patrol!

Quick, we must find somewhere to hide!

Who's that?

Ha! ha! ha! ha! *He! he! he! he!* *Ho! ho! ho! ho!*

OOOOH! . . . *Terrific!*

Well? What about that, eh?

Wooah! Wooah! *Quiet, Snowy, quiet!*

That was a close shave, Captain.
Yes! . . . Lucky for us we had all day yesterday to practise! Poor Senhor Oliveira!

Pitchers? . . . I'm so sorry, ma'am, my stock is completely exhausted . . .

Good! Now we're out of the city.
And there's the well . . . Confound it, he promised us there'd be no one about at this hour!

صباح آلخير دمتّحمك آآخير يا آآتَر

لا تراداوالى نمكن
?

لمننا ننايف دفسكك وهى بينى وحمك
?

! ?

Why can't you talk English like everyone else, you fancy-dress Fatima?! What do you want, anyway?

WOOAH!

Billions of blue blistering barnacles! That old witch will raise the alarm! . . .

. . . And our guide isn't here! . . . Oliveira was quite definite that he'd wait near the well, with the horses . . . Now what is it, Snowy?

Wooah! . . . Wooah! . . .

There he is! Fine! Back in the saddle again . . .

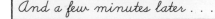

And a few minutes later . . .

My stirrups, blistering barnacles! . . . My stirrups! . . .

Meanwhile . . .

Hello, Colonel Achmed? . . . This is Mull Pasha at Sheik Bab El Ehr's headquarters . . . Order your Mosquitoes to take off immediately . . . Hello? . . . Yes. Their mission: to wipe out a party of three horsemen who have left Wadesdah, heading for the Jebel . . . You understand? . . . Good . . . Armoured cars are already on the way . . . Hello? . . . Yes, they are partisans of Ben Kalish Ezab . . . Yes, wipe them out.

There they are! . . . Fire!

26

ZZZZ

HALT!

Friends! . . . Friends! . . . Don't shoot!

Friends? . . . We will soon see . . . Give the password!

The camels bark . . . er, no . . . The dogs bark and the camels pass.

Good . . . Come forward. Who are these strangers?

Friends of Ben Kalish Ezab. They have travelled far to see him.

That is good. We will take them before him.

These holes in the rock? . . . Yes, I noticed them. They look like windows. It wouldn't surprise me if there were people living inside.

Nonsense! They couldn't possibly. Still, we'll soon find out . . .

Living in there! That's a good one!

لحمّ شي ذزيد اكك شويّيت ماء

Beg pardon, ma'am!

All right. People do live there . . .

I . . . Oh, look there!

28

Thundering typhoons! . . . A Roman temple, hewn from the rock! . . . Incredible!

We have arrived.

A few minutes later . . .

How stupendous! An entire city carved out of the mountain.

Tintin! . . . Captain! . . . You here? . . . It is unbelievable!

And my son? . . . My own little treasure? My precious darling . . . Where is he?

Ah, yes . . . We left him at Marlinspike, Your Highness. But rest assured, he is in good hands.

Poor little lamb! How sad he must be, so far from his Papa.

And now I'll leave you tied to the palm tree, so the crocodiles can come and eat you. Ha! ha! We're having fun, aren't we, Nestor? . . .

Confounded brat! . . . Ah, someone's coming. They'll set me free.

Ah, Nestor, I was looking for you. Could you give me a hand? It's nothing much: simply give me a little push.

Mmmm! . . . Mmm!

It's to test the new steering mechanism I've fitted to my roller-skates . . . Quite simple, really. They use the same principle for steering model cars.

Mmm! . . . Mm!

For instance, at the moment, my skates are locked right over to the left . . . If someone were to push me now I should turn round more or less on the same spot.

Mmm! . . . Mmm!

But I'm quite sure that despite his sadness my cherub is a little ray of sunshine, bringing life and gaiety into your old home.

Undoubtedly!

And you, what brings you here? . . . Come along in and sit down. You must be tired. And you'll certainly be hungry and thirsty. I will have some refreshments brought to you.

Well, Your Highness, we are here to try and help you; also, to get to the bottom of a mystery, in which Arabair seem to have an important part.

Arabair? The dogs! . . . They will pay dearly for their treachery . . . I gave them permission to establish a base at Wadesdah, an important link on the route to Mecca . . .

One day, about three months ago, my little Abdullah, my flawless jewel, expressed a wish to see the Arabair planes loop the loop a few times before landing at Wadesdah . . .

Loop the loop!? But . . Highness . . .

Nothing simpler, don't you agree? . . . And it would have given my lambkin such pleasure! . . . Well, instead of seizing this opportunity of pleasing my little sugar-plum, they refused, on some trumped-up excuse . . .

But Highness . . .

Naturally, I was very angry and threatened to terminate our agreement. I also used another threat: that I would reveal to the world that Arabair are involved in slave trading.

WHAT? . . .

GRRR . . .

Slave trading, no less . . . Their planes touching down at Wadesdah on the way from Africa are always full to bursting with native Sudanese and Senegalese. These are Mohammedan converts, making their pilgrimage to Mecca.

Yes, go on . . .

On the other hand, on the return journey their planes are mostly empty . . . Why? . . . Because somewhere between Wadesdah and Mecca these unfortunate negroes are sold as slaves.

But that's frightful!

Er . . . Yes . . . But to get back to Arabair: these jackals stirred up trouble in my country, and thanks to their support, the accursed Bab El Ehr was able to seize power . . . But it won't be for long . . . I'll throw him out, that mangy dog, that stinking hyena, that slimy serpent, that . . .

GRAOW

By Allah! . . . Let us hope your dog hasn't gone near Ayesha!

GRRAOW

?

?

!

CRACK

GRAOW

Achmed! . . . Quick! . . . Ayesha!

Hello! . . . You here too? . . .

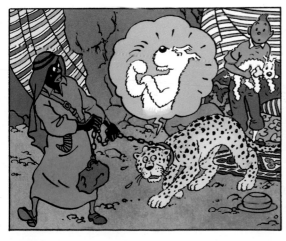

Yes, a tame cheetah. But you see what happens when he is annoyed . . . And I am the same: woe betide those who attack me . . . The perfidious Bab El Ehr will learn this one day, to his cost!

GRRR! . . .

. . . And that infamous di Gorgonzola, too, the owner of Arabair.

Arabair belongs to di Gorgonzola?

It does indeed. Di Gorgonzola – shipping magnate, newspaper proprietor, radio, television and cinema tycoon, air-line king, dealer in pearls, gun-runner, trafficker in slaves – the man who helped Bab El Ehr to seize power . . . But patience! Ill-gotten gains benefit no one!

That's what he thinks!

He's an international crook; he must be put out of harm's way.

Yes, you are right. But what can we do to expose his dreadful traffic in slaves?

Tell me, Your Highness . . . Mecca is the terminus for Arabair, isn't it? . . . Good . . . Is there any way of actually getting us there?

Aha! . . . More and more interesting!

To Mecca? That's not easy at the moment. But if you will give me two or three days, I will find means of putting you aboard a sailing-ship, which will take you there.

Thank you, Highness.

Aha! This will please Bab El Ehr...

GRAOW!

Again? What has happened now?

It is Ben Yussef, O Master... Ayesha jumped on him... See, it will be at least three weeks before he is well... It seems that he trod on Ayesha's tail...

Oh, poor creature!

Three days later...

There, everything is arranged. You leave tomorrow at dawn, with two trusted men. They will lead you to a point on the coast where a small vessel will be waiting to take you to Mecca. But be on your guard. Di Gorgonzola is a dangerous man.

Two days have passed...

Here we are... You may dismount ... But stay while I make sure that the boat has arrived.

He's signalling to us... We can go.

Ah, so that's the tub we're going to board. It's a dhow... No; I beg your pardon: a sambuk.

Look, they have just put a boat out.

Danger! Danger! A mounted patrol!

By the beard of the Prophet, something suspicious is going on over there.

Halt! ... Who goes there?

By Allah! ... They have stumbled on a patrol! ...

Ha! ha! ha! Soldiers? Them? ... Don't make me laugh! One shot into the air and they bolted like rabbits!

At dawn ...

Ha! ha! ha! ha!

Ha! ha! ha! I was thinking of those twopenny-halfpenny coastguards galloping headlong! Anyone'd think they were trying to break the sound barrier!

Unfortunately they'll have made a report ... In which case ...

What a pessimist you are! What are you afraid of? ... That they'll send a squadron of battleships after us?

Not that, certainly, but ...

But what?

Over there, Captain! ... That's just what I feared!

Thundering typhoons! Mosquitoes!

They're coming back! ... This is going to be hot! ... Everybody down!

Meanwhile . . .

May I have the pleasure of this samba, Princess?

But of course, Marquis.

What an ideal yacht for a cruise!

The "Scheherazade" is certainly a wonderful ship . . . And what a good idea to have a fancy-dress ball on board . . . Ma-a-arvellous!

Excuse me, my lord, there is a radio call for you . . . It's urgent . . .

Very well, I'm coming.

You see, dear lady? Business, always business. I am indeed a slave . . . Will you forgive me?

Don't give it a thought.

What an entrancing host he is. This cruise aboard the "Scheherazade" is really too enchanting!

Yes, he's a true gentleman. Naturally, malicious tongues spread rumours that he has a shady past . . .

It's only to be expected that such luxury arouses envy. One must admit . . .

Hello! Hello! K6VM calling R3KO . . . Transmit in code . . . Over.

Powerful insects have stung the blue goat. Parasites 1 and 2 are in the bag. Out.

K6VM to R3KO. Understood. Out.

Good . . . Now for the book, and we'll decode this. Parasites 1 and 2 – I know who they are!

There . . . I have it . . . Excellent! Mull Pasha has done well. We're rid of those two meddlers!

If this goes on, Captain, we'll soon be on Dr Bombard's diet: plankton and sea-water.

Marquis! . . . Yoohoo, Marquis!

Marquis, where are you?

Here! What is it?

Castaways, my dear fellow! Out there on a raft.

It's true, Marquis. Real castaways! How madly gay!

Yes, yes, I know . . . I . . . I've just given orders for the Captain to pick them up.

Oh, how gorgeous! I've always dreamed of seeing real castaways!

They're going about!

Saved!

They've seen us at last!

Saved! . . . Oh, ♪♪ what a beautiful morning!

That does it. Now this really is the Raft of the Medusa!

By Lucifer! What's to be done? They mustn't see me!

Hello? Yes, my lord Marquis . . . Your name's not to be mentioned in front of the castaways . . . Yes, m'lord.

In addition, I want you to remove these men at once – my guests are too inquisitive, and must have no contact with them.

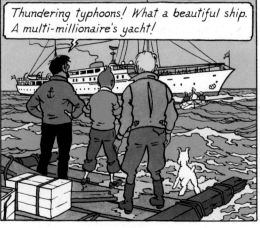

Thundering typhoons! What a beautiful ship. A multi-millionaire's yacht!

And those fools think their troubles are over! Ha! ha! ha! That's a good joke!

Thundering typhoons! What a magnificent yacht! Whose is she? . . . Hey, are they having a carnival on board?

Almost . . . A fancy-dress ball . . . And what a bunch they are: high society, I can tell you; nothing but dukes, duchesses and film stars - all the nobs.

Per la Madonna! Can you believe it! . . . It's Tintin, and his friend the deep-sea fisherman, Paddock.

I must go and welcome them. Art must embrace the children of Adventure!

In the name of the Marquis di Gorgonzola welcome aboard, carissime mie!

Signora Castafiore! . . . Run for it! What shall we do? . . . Hop back on the raft?

My dear Tintin!

Delighted to see you again, my dear Padlock . . . er . . . Harrock.

. . . 'n roll, Signora Castoroili, Harrock'n-roll!

I'm so sorry, Signora, but his lordship has given orders: these poor men are completely exhausted. And then . . . there's the risk of infection, you know.

But my good man, I'm not ill!

A little later . . .

Well, Parker, have you questioned them?

Yes, m'lord. They were aboard a sambuk, being taken to Mecca . . .

. . . This morning, their boat was machine-gunned and set on fire by aircraft from Khemed. After shooting down one of the planes, they made themselves a raft. They then rescued the pilot of the aircraft.

Well done, Parker. Thank you.

If your lordship will pardon me, I think I should mention that Signora Castafiore, who knows the two castaways, welcomed them in your lordship's name.

Diavolo!

The Marquis di Gorgonzola's yacht! . . . It's fantastic . . . I must be dreaming.

Come on, Tintin . . . Up in the clouds again? . . . Hey! Tintin!

They can't stay here on board. But what's to be done? What indeed? ... Ah, I have it! The "Ramona". ... She's in these waters ... Tomorrow we must pass one another, as if by chance.

Get dressed quickly. You're in luck. We've met a merchantman bound for Mecca: just where you were making for. Her master has agreed to take you aboard.

Er . . . I . . . What . . . Good, that's fine.

So that's that! And now, my fine friends, I wish you a pleasant journey. Ha! ha! ha! ha!

Ah, this is the place for me: back aboard a good old freighter.

There, you two: these are your quarters. Your pal's going elsewhere . . . The skipper will be down to see you soon: he'll bring you your whisky himself!

Hi, you lubberly scum, not so fast! What do you mean?

This is too much! He's locked us in, the insolent porcupine!

Open up! Thundering typhoons, open up! You ill-mannered savages!

THUMP   THUMP

Well, well, you old drunkard! So you're kicking up a row already?

Allan!!

Wreckers! . . . Pirates! . . . Filibusters! . . . Picaroons! Leaving us in the lurch on a doomed ship! To Davy Jones with the lot of you!

Follow me . . . We'll probably find a raft up for'ard.

We obviously have a vocation for shipwrecks!

HEY! HELP! HELP!

EFFENDI! EFFENDI!

There's someone in the hold! . . . What the . . . ?!

Who are you, below there?

We good black men . . . Want come out . . . No can breathe . . . We afraid . . .

Negroes! A lot of them, too, I'd say . . . What shall we do, Captain? We can't just abandon them.

You're right. Come on.

We'll try and put out the blaze . . . That cargo . . . I just can't make it out!

Eighteen tons of high explosive and ammunition: it'll make a pretty fireworks display!

That's it! The hose is connected . . . Now then, let's open the valve.

Blub . . . I . . . blub . . . I've got it, Cap . . . blub . . .

Thanks . . . that's it . . . I'll tackle the fire . . . You go over to port and get another hose into action.

Let's hope this will do the job!

What about the explosion? Is it due for today or . . . But . . . but . . . I can't see any more smoke or flames!

By thunder! The fire's gone out! Put her about boys. We're going back.

It . . . it's out . . . A huge wave . . . I was very nearly washed overboard . . .

What luck! . . . Now for those poor fellows below, Captain.

You're right, but first of all . . .

. . . I'm going to try to restart the engines. You go up on the bridge and take the wheel.

Half an hour later . . .

By thunder! . . . The "Ramona" is drawing away! . . . Someone has got her engines going!

Phew! that was no joke, alone; but she's under way at last.

Magnificent, Captain . . . And now for the Negroes.

There's something more urgent: to send out a distress call by radio.

! OH!

Look!

Skut! . . . Dead?

No, he's alive . . . See, he's coming round.

Skut! Skut, old man, say something! What happened?

You escape! Hurry! . . . Hurry! . . . The fire! . . . Ship full of ammunition! . . . Hurry before explosion . . .

Ammunition! The pirates! . . . That's why they deserted like rats . . .

Don't worry, Skut: the fire's out. There's no more danger . . . But what about you? What happened?

They wake me, to go with them . . . Without you . . . I refuse . . . I want to . . . er . . . wake you . . . and send radio signal.

Then they are angry . . . Break radio and fight with me . . . Then I . . . knocked-out. They go?

Yes, they abandoned us, the iconoclasts. So here we are alone on board, with a crowd of Negroes in the hold.

You like . . . I can help you . . . Repair radio, perhaps, send S.O.S. . . .

Good idea . . . Do that . . . I'm going to make sure there's no further danger.

A little later . . .

No more need to worry, youngster: the fire is right out.

Now I'll take care of those Negroes. First, to let them out . . .

Save poor Muslim!

Me ill. Me dying.

All right! I'm coming now!

Hey there! . . . Let go of me!! . . . HELP, TINTIN! . . . HELP! HELP!

?

Troglodytes! . . . Sea-gherkins! . . . Pickled herrings! Leave me alone!

Back, visigoths! . . . Back, anacoluthons!

!

Hang on, Captain! . . . I'm coming! . . .

47

So it is! A sambuk . . . The harbour pilot from Jidda, perhaps . . . No, we're still too far from shore . . . A fisherman, then?

How odd . . . he's signalling to us . . . We'll heave to, and see what he wants . . .

Salaams, O sailor . . . Captain Allan is up there?

Captain Allan? . . . Finished . . . Gone . . . I am captain now.

Ah, you have replaced him . . . Good, good . . . Is the coke of best quality this time?

The coke?? Again? Blistering barnacles, what's all this nonsense about coke? Thundering typhoons, there's no coke on board!

No coke on board! . . . Ha! ha! ha!

Come here, you.

Yes, Effendi.

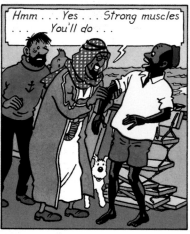

Hmm . . . Yes . . . Strong muscles . . . You'll do . . .

And teeth? . . . Come on, open your mouth . . . Hmm, not too bad . . . Teeth quite sound . . .

Here, have you quite finished playing the cattle-dealer? This man's not a horse, nor a slave . . .

Ssh! . . . You mustn't say that! . . . "Coke" is the word, as you well know.

Coke!! . . . Blistering barnacles! . . . Tintin was right! There still are slave-traders . . . And that's what you're up to, you brute!

You trafficker in human flesh! You deserve to be strung up on the mizzen yardarm!

LOOK OUT!

ZZINNG

You cut-throat, you! . . . You're lucky I don't stuff your beard down your gullet! . . . But get out . . . viper! And take care that you don't cross my path again!

Sheer off, filibuster! . . . Out of my sight, you gallows bird!

Baboon! . . . Carpet-seller! . . . Paranoiac! . . . Pockmark! . . . Cannibal!

Duck-billed platypus! . . . Jellied-eel! . . . Bashi-bazouk! . . . Anthropophagus! . . . Cercopithecus! Psychopath! . . . Er . . .

No good, Captain. He's too far away now . . .

That's what you think! He hasn't heard the last of me!

Where now?

On to the bridge.

PIRATE! ECTOPLASM COELACANTH VULTURE!

BODY-SNATCHER! OSTROGOTH! VANDAL!

This time I think he really is out of earshot.

Yes! . . . More's the pity . . . dirty slave-trader!

By the way . . . How did you tumble to the word "coke"?

I'll show you.

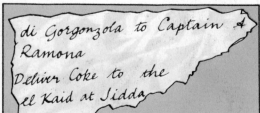

I found this scrap of paper on the table while you were plotting our course on the chart. Read it.

di Gorgonzola to Captain of Ramona
Deliver Coke to the
el Kaid at Jidda

By the beard of the Prophet, the dog will pay dearly for this!

Emyny sofoyi ooiboo-yi konychéeré!

Yirō!

Beyni!

Loyotō!

?

Now then . . . What's going on? . . . Why all the quarrelling?

I not want to go to Mecca. I tell them you are good white man, you speak truth. I remember in my village three young men went to Mecca . . . Two years ago . . . They not come back . . . They no doubt slaves . . . I not want to go to Mecca! . . . I not want to be slave.

Me too, I not go.

Me too!

Good, so I haven't preached in vain! . . . All right, we'll make a bargain: those who don't want to go to Mecca will be landed at another port. As for the rest, they can continue the voyage if they want to . . .

Good, Effendi.

The next morning . . .

There . . . the day after tomorrow we'll be at Djibouti, and that'll be the end of our worries . . .

Yes, if all goes well! I shan't be really happy till we get there. You can bet that at this very moment di Gorgonzola is aware of the situation. And he knows that we know . . . Watch out for what he's cooking up! . . .

BRRRRR

?

!

An aeroplane . . . They're circling us . . . how odd . . .

Hello, hello . . . Albatross to Shark . . . Have sighted Ramona 20 miles west of the Farasan Islands . . . She is steering south-south-east. Over.

Hello, hello . . . Shark to Albatross . . . Message received . . . Steering west . . .

. . . to intercept her . . . Out.

Aha! My orders have been carried out.

He's going off . . . I wonder what he was up to.

I don't know, but I don't much care for that sort of visit.

The trap is closing: my boys are on the job! . . . In a few hours the "Ramona" will have disappeared, with crew and cargo . . . So all the incriminating evidence will be effectively liquidated.

That plane snooping around worries me . . . If I were you, Captain, I'd alter course.

You're right . . . I'll do so.

Well, Skut, how's the radio? Working?

No . . .

No! . . . The radio not working . . . I not find the trouble . . . I not know what more to do . . .

BRRRR

Again? . . .

The same one? . . .

Be careful, the wire!

OH!

?

The radio! Quite all broken now!

!

?

Hello . . . Albatross to Shark . . . Have found Ramona again.

Steering due south; she is 30 miles east of Dahlak-kebir Island.

That bird of ill-omen is getting on my nerves.

Buzz off, you stool-pigeon! You're asking for a smack on the nose!

!

Shark to Albatross. Ramona in sight. Preparing to dive.

I say, Skut, I'm terribly sorry! You've worked for so long on the radio . . . and then I'm so clumsy . . .

Ssh!

She working! . . . She working now!

What?! . . . After a bang like that? It's not possible.

She working, I tell you! Listen . . .

!

BEEP-BEEP-BEEP

Captain! . . . Captain! . . . The radio! . . . It's going!!

I . . . So sorry, but the radio, Captain . . . The radio . . . It's going!!

Oh yes? Where? . . . I hope it steers clear of me . . .

. . . because I've had enough of being rammed! Only a couple of minutes ago, plop – a flying-fish slap in my face. And now you: that's enough!

Flying fish? I must have a look at them with my binoculars.

Oh, how beautiful! You'd think they were little silver arrows . . .

Look at them, skimming over the waves . . . I can see two . . . no, three . . .

And there . . . Hey, what in the world's that?

CAPTAIN! . . . CAPTAIN! . . . A PERISCOPE!

Where is it now? . . . I can't see it any more . . . But I'm absolutely sure . . .

Now then, keep calm . . .

There, Captain, over there, I'm sure . . . Right out there . . . I saw the wake, I tell you . . .

Now keep calm, young shaver! Periscope or no periscope, keep calm . . .

Ten thousand thundering typhoons! A periscope! . . . There! . . . It's true! . . .

Action stations! . . . Fire! . . . S.O.S. . . . The radio, Skat! Confound! the radio, Skut! . . . Send for help! At once! . . . A submarine! . . . Clear the decks for action! . . . Keep calm! Don't panic! . . . Women and children first!

Calm down, Captain, calm down! . . . All isn't lost yet!

You're right . . . Keep cool . . . keep calm and don't panic!

Disaster! . . . The end! . . . There's nothing we can do! If they're di Gorgonzola's people we're finished!

But why?

The ammunition! . . . In the forward hold . . . A torpedo in there, and you know the rest!

Of course! Only the torpedo isn't here yet! Come on, hurry; everyone on the alert.

Not far away . . .

We're almost within range . . . They don't know what's in store for them.

This won't take long to settle . . . Stand by No. 1 tube . . .

Tintin at the radio. You at the wheel, Skut. Repeat my orders when I give them. Remember, starboard is right; port on the left . . .

S.O.S. . . . S.O.S. . . . s.s. Ramona calling. Unidentified submarine in immediate vicinity. . . . We fear the worst . . . Here is our position.

No. 1 tube, fire!

S.O.S. . . . S.O.S. . . . s.s. Ramona calling . . . In danger of being torpedoed . . .

Torpedo to port! Hard a starboard! . . .

Hard a starboard it is!

Curses on them! They've swung away . . . They must have spotted us.

S.O.S. . . . S.O.S. . . . A torpedo has just missed us . . . S.O.S. . . . Hurry please . . . S.O.S.

A moment later, aboard the U.S.S. Los Angeles . . .

An S.O.S. I just picked up, sir.

What's all this ballyhoo about a submarine? . . . There isn't a war on, is there?

But meanwhile . . .

Starboard 20 . . . Ahead, speed six knots . . . Stand by No. 2 tube.

Hooray! Someone's heard our call!

U.S.S. Los Angeles to s.s. Ramona. Your S.O.S. received. We are coming to your assistance. Will be with you in three hours.

We've managed to miss the first torpedo, but we'll probably be done for before you get here.

There they are ahead, to port. This time they won't escape us . . .

By rights he should be astern, to starboard. In a few minutes I'll turn to port again, to confuse him.

Peer sport 30° . . . I mean steer port 30°.

Port 30° it is.

By the powers of Satan! They've dodged us again!

Wait now! He'll end up by turning to starboard again . . . And then . . .

Submarine obviously belongs to the slave-traders. Their leader is the Marquis di Gorgonzola, now aboard m.s. Scheherazade, cruising in the Red Sea.

Starboard 45°.

Starboard 45° it is.

Right! . . . No. 2 tube, fire!

Torpedo to starboard! Thundering typhoons! Quick, the engine-room telegraph . . .

Blistering barnacles! Full speed ahead!

Billions of blue blistering barnacles!

Thundering typhoons! The engine-room telegraph is jammed at half-speed astern. Quick, a screw-driver!

By Lucifer! They're going astern . . . our torpedo has missed again . . . They're tough, those boys . . .

Hooray! It's passed ahead of us.

S.O.S. A second torpedo has just missed. Hurry, Los Angeles.

Quick! Quick! I must release this infernal machine!

PCHKRAAPRVT! . . . TRRKHKRAA! . . . You confounded rattletrap . . .

. . . tin-can contraption! . . . Take that!

YEEOWW!

Ah, they're still going astern! Very well! No. 3 and No. 4 tubes ready?

CLING
CLANG

Take that, you slot-machine, you!

?

Hello? . . . Engine room? . . . Hello?

Hello, Effendi?

BRROM

Too late! . . . They've got us!

56

BRROM!

Again!

No, they're depth charges! . . . Whew! I really thought we'd been torpedoed . . .

U.S. Navy seaplanes, with those pirates for a target! . . . They're certainly machines from the Los Angeles.

Oho! Great grandfathers! What a pasting! . . . They'll be as flat as a Dover sole after that!

Wait! . . . There, that upheaval in the water . . .

Look! The submarine has surfaced!

Yes . . . Obviously they've been badly knocked about . . .

Victory! . . . They're waving a white flag . . . They're surrendering . . . The game's up.

Hello, hello. Unidentified submarine: remain on the surface and stop your engines. One suspicious move and we'll blow you out of the water . . .

Torpedoes are out of the question now . . . A limpet-mine on their hull! . . . With the ammunition aboard, it'll look like an accident . . . In you go: you've plenty of time: the mine's set to explode in one hour.

Be quick: they're coming back!

Go!

What a job!

Saved! Yippee! Saved!

Hooray!

Tralalala-laika!

That is white man's folk-dance.

They said the ammunition was in the forepart . . .

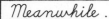

Meanwhile . . .

This is all very fine, but we must wait for the Los Angeles. I'm going to see if there's any chance of dropping anchor.

Twenty-two fathoms depth . . . that's perfect . . .

Ahoy, there! Let go the anchor! Eighty fathoms of chain.

GLOOP

HIC   HIC   HIC   HIC   HIC

An hour later . . .

Hooray! . . . There she is! . . . The Los Angeles!

American cruiser in sight!

Don't worry, boys . . . She'll blow up any moment now.

HIC
BOOOM

? ? ? ? ?

Billions of bilious blue blistering barnacles in a thundering typhoon! Another joke by that infernal child . . . Shall I never be left in peace?! In peace!!

Sir, Mr Wagg has just arrived . . .

Who? . . . Jolyon Wagg? . . . Oh, no, no! . . . I want some peace! . . . Peace!

Hello, old boy! How are you, you old sea-dog? I'm doing fine . . . in the pink! . . . Ha! ha! ha! . . . What a lark to see you again, you old humbug, you!

Er . . .

Well, my old salt, I've got a surprise for you . . . I know the country's pretty, but it's dull as ditchwater . . .

A matter of taste . . .

No, no, take it from me, it's dull. So I said to myself: "Jolyon," I said, "you must go and liven things up for that old stick-in-the-mud . . ."

That's very kind of you, but . . .

Now, now, turn it up! No buts! Too easy. I'm president of the Vagabond Car Club down my way; all I've had to do is organise a rally, and the final trials . . .

. . . are at Marlinspike!

THE END